Dedication

To all those women out there who believe that true love does exist and won't give up until they find it.

To my son Jake, who made me realize how precious life is with, or without a man in your life.

To my husband Neil, who is proof that there are still "good ones" left, and that finding the right partner is worth the wait.

Frogs, Frogs, Introduction, Frogs, Frogs...

I suppose that if we could orchestrate whom we are to be with throughout our entire lives, and it always worked out the way we envisioned it, that life may be a bit boring. Whether predictability is boring, or not, we really have no choice. In the end, I believe, it is all left up to fate. I was living a life that I had pretty much planned as a little girl, (castle and excessive riches excluded), but at a young age, things just seemed to work out the "way that they were supposed to". Then all of a sudden, (well, ok maybe within about a year), I turned around and realized that my life and my husband were not at all what I thought they were. This curveball totally threw me for a loop.

Getting a divorce was nothing I could have prepared myself for. Failure at a marriage was definitely not in my plan. After a fair amount of grieving, feelings of anger, rejection, and heartache, I realized that it was really over, and that I would have to move on.

I was 31, a single mother and unemployed. I was thrown into a 180 degree life changing reality; and being single again was the scariest thing I'd ever faced.

I managed to find work as a Graphic Designer and Art Director, (the field I had briefly left when my son was born). Working long hours and finding childcare was certainly not easy or ideal, but I didn't have a choice. I made the best of it. I was fortunate to find a nanny who was a Godsend. I cherished the fact that I was lucky to have a wonderful son, and worked hard to have a good life for us both.

I was determined to look at my new life as a new beginning and not to dwell on the past. This meant getting myself "out there" in whatever ways possible. Enter the world of summer share houses, winter share houses, parties, blind dates, singles events, athletic challenges, temple functions, and yes, the inevitable online dating. It all seemed a bit overwhelming. I became tired just thinking about it!

In order to get through it all while maintaining a smile on my face, I managed to see the humor and amusement of my experiences. So, although I admit that I often came home from many dates thinking that joining a convent may be a better option, I somehow managed to get back on the horse again, and again...and again.

What I Learned

I learned that dating is like interviewing, and when one opportunity doesn't work out, you just have to try for the next one. I learned that you cannot force things to happen when they aren't meant to, no matter how badly you want them to. I learned that there are a lot of bad men out here. I learned that there are a lot of good men out there.

I learned that you have to be honest with others and especially you must be honest with yourself.

I learned that men generally are from Mars and that we just have to accept that. I learned that the best way to get over a man who has broken your heart is to meet another.

I learned that you should not bank on others to fix you up with the perfect man, they mean well but it's still a crapshoot. I learned that a man's interpretation of "time" and a woman's version are very different.

I learned to go with my first gut instinct---it's usually right.

I learned that men typically like long hair and fit bodies. I learned that a gentleman is a rare gem. I learned that there is no perfect situation and that you must make decisions and prioritize your values for yourself.

I learned that you have to kiss a lot of frogs.

I share my dating experiences with you in the hope that you can relate to some of my tales, that you can laugh with me, that you can hopefully see the glass half-full, and most of all, that you realize how important it is to feel good about your life and love yourself before you can begin to love someone else. A strong woman exudes confidence; and that is always attractive.

I share with you my adventures from the Frog Pond.

Frog #1:
The arrogant frog

You mean I actually go up to strange men and talk to them?

I was thrilled to be invited along a business trip to a beautiful island by a friend. It was just what I needed to get out of my slump and start fresh. After spending my first day alone tanning myself, I decided to ditch my book and wander down to the singles beach club that was just down the beach. This type of behavior was completely foreign to me. I wasn't even exactly sure what I would do when I got there. I soon realized that the combination of bikinis, sun, and white sandy beaches are useful in meeting men. I managed to meet my first attraction in the water---wow this was easier than I thought---and actually kind of fun!

He and his friends snuck me into the club for lunch and drinks, and later I met up with him for dinner. After I came back home to reality, he actually wanted to come visit me! Amazing, I never thought I would meet someone this quickly.

He was extremely complimentary to me on the island and also during our phone calls back home. He was also eager to meet up again.

Unfortunately, the visit didn't go as well as I thought it would. Not only was he not able to "perform" but he also turned out to be very critical and actually had the nerve to insult the place where I lived---what a jerk!

Positives:

My self-esteem was built up again---I'm still attracted to the opposite sex, and they are attracted to me---what a relief!

Negatives:

My first sexual experience since being with my husband for 12 years, and the guy has "equipment failure"---please tell me this isn't happening!

What I learned:

It definitely wasn't me.

Frog #2

The confused frog

There are a lot of cute skiers, this is actually fun!

After I got over the long ride to the ski house and the fact that I would be sharing a bathroom with 10 other people (yuck!), I settled into my "shared" room and met this guy at the house before we even went out. He was cute, and easy to be with, (at first). We hung out for the weekend and then continued seeing each other back home. We ended up dating for several months. Being a single mom living in the "burbs", I would usually meet my dates in the city. So I came in on several occasions to see him. Being the type of eater that I am, (I love all kinds of food and absolutely love to eat good food), I begrudgingly accepted that this guy was Kosher. Who am I to judge someone else's beliefs? This was, unfortunately, the first sign that this was not going to work out. As the dating went on, he began to tell me of his desire to expand his religious beliefs and way of life. I applauded his dedication, and although this was not the type of lifestyle that I wanted, I figured I'd hang out with him a little longer. Well, that ended soon enough when he told me that although I am Jewish (reformed), I was not "Jewish enough" for him. How could I argue with that? I was not going to wear a wig, long skirts and pray every day… so I guess he was right! I actually gave him a lot of credit for following his belief and pursuing a life that he thought would make him happy…that is, until I found out a year later he married a "shiksa"!* Go figure.

Positives:
He was a nice guy and he meant well.

Negatives:
He hadn't "found himself" yet--it was a problem.

What I learned:
Many people are generally very confused.

Side Note: Size actually does matter.

* Shiksa: A non-Jewish girl or woman

Frog #3

The nerdy frog

This guy in this personal ad sounds great...

There are times when you want to crawl under the table and be invisible...this was one of those times. No need to expand any further on this person.

Positives:
None.

Negatives:
I now know where the word "nerd" came from.

What I learned:
People generally lie when describing themselves in a personal ad. Never agree to dinner on a blind date...drinks only!

Frog #4

The boring frog

Sometimes you just have to go with the flow....

This one was a friend of my friend's boyfriend. We met for a drink, it wasn't too painful, but not interesting enough to do again.

Positives:
A very nice guy.

Negatives:
It just wasn't there for me.

What I learned:
Sometimes you're not sure why it "clicks" for you or why it doesn't.

Frog #5
The spiritual frog

You have to be open-minded....

We were set up through a friend. I'm still not sure what it was that attracted me to him, but I ended up seeing him on and off for 2 years. He was a little older than I was, and divorced with teenagers. I was newly divorced, newly hurt, and not confident enough to have a casual relationship, which is what he apparently wanted. I tried to be casual, but I always seemed to want something more, more than he was able or wanted to give. Although he was a great guy, he was soooo not right for me. I was very vulnerable and needy at the time and he was the one who was there. The funny thing is, that later on, after I became more confident with myself and became an "expert dater," I ended up meeting several guys (i.e.: frog # 6) whom were like I was at this point. Timing is everything.

Positives:

He was a good, caring person who helped me through the nastiness of my divorce and the adjustment of being a single parent. We had fun. He was a great cook, (don't ever take that for granted!).

Negatives:

We were never right for each other.

What I learned:

Sometimes you get so caught up in wanting to be with someone that you lose sight of why you want to be with them in the first place. You can't fit a square peg in a round hole.

Frog #6
The needy frog

I just know you're going to like this one....

A set-up through another friend. We dated for a few weeks. I had to break it off. He wasn't confident enough…My how the tables had turned!

Positives:

Cute, great guy.

Negatives:

Too newly separated, too needy.

What I learned:

Timing is everything.

Frog #7

The sexy frog

Much of what you hear about a summer beach house is actually true.

We met in the share house. I was warned not to get involved with him. I didn't listen. The fling lasted through the summer, and I admit that it was fun, but it never went anywhere beyond that, or I, for sure, would have had my heart broken.

Positives:
Cute and sexy---he was the bad boy that everyone wants be with just once, or twice, or...

Negatives:
Player. Player. Player.

What I learned:
Sometimes you should listen to your friends.

Frog #8

The tadpole

-You actually can be too young or too thin -

The sunburn, the music, the drinking, the moonlight...

We met in a bar at the beach. I hung out with him for the evening until I snapped back into reality...wait a minute, this guy is really too young for me.

Positives:
It's a confidence boost when younger men are attracted to you.

Negatives:
I tried my first cigarette before he was born.

What I learned:
It's ok to "slip up" every now and then as long as nobody gets hurt.

Frog #9

The pretentious frog

I should have known he was not my type.

One of the guys "in the scene" from the beach house. I figured I'd give it a shot—what's the harm in one more date???

Positives:

No time wasted—it was a lunch date, (you have to eat anyway).

Negatives:

You can't help but wonder why sometimes a guy isn't interested in you. Did I have salad stuck in my teeth? Was I just a boring lunch date? You usually never find out.

What I learned:

There is big hole that some men fall into, never to be seen or heard from again.

Frog #10

The skier frog

Thank God I ski.

What girl isn't a sucker for a man who plays the guitar and sings? How could I resist? He was a super nice guy, just bad timing or not quite right, or something like that. Oh well, time to move on.

Positives:
Cute, sweet, nice guy.

Negatives:
It never progressed.

What I learned:
It's ok to just have fun and enjoy the moment without taking everything too seriously.

Frog #11

The egotistical frog

This is getting exhausting.

This was a set-up by a friend. One that I was pleasantly surprised by. Wow, this could be a match made in heaven! We both had one child the same age, and were actually mutually attracted. We even met each other's families. Although I enjoyed being with him, after a few months I decided to end it after realizing that he would never make me happy, because his first priority was himself.

Positives:
Very cute, I think he meant well.

Negatives:
It's a bad sign when a guy takes longer to get ready that you do.

What I learned:
I never want to be with someone who always thinks of himself first.

Frog #12
The handsome frog

Some blind dates turn out to be nice surprises.

He was tall, good-looking, good personality, successful…I really liked him. We were off to a great start. We were very attracted to one another and he seemed fun...until about 2 months into dating when it suddenly all derailed. I'm not quite sure exactly what happened, but the relationship was just not moving forward so I broke it off.

Positives:
I enjoyed being with him while it lasted.

Negatives:
I guess not everybody is going to be into you…you just have to accept it.

What I learned:
You learn when it's just not happening, and you just have to break it off, take your losses and move on.

Side Note:
He later married a much older celebrity who shall remain nameless.

Frog #13

The "game player" frog

I just knew he wasn't for me.

My friend insisted on fixing me up with a guy whom I was a little unsure of. He actually turned out to be fun to be with, and ridiculously nice to me. The caveat was...I was not physically attracted to him. He was extremely persistent though, and wined and dined me so much that eventually he started to grow on me. So would you believe that as soon as I started getting into him, he ditched me! Go figure!

Positives:

Flying on a private jet is pretty cool (I may never get to do that again). It's nice to be spoiled every once in a while.

Negatives:

He worked so hard trying to win me over, yet once he did, he didn't want me anymore....What is that all about?

What I learned:

Men who are just looking for a challenge do not have the integrity of the type of person that I was looking for.

Frog #14

The nameless frog

They all started to blend into the same shade of green.

I don't remember, but I know it was someone.

Positives:
I got out of the house.

Negatives:
I'm sure I could've used that baby-sitting money towards a new pair of shoes instead.

What I learned:
I should have been taking notes all along, because someday I may write a book about all this...

Frog #15

The cute frog

Ok, so I get the allure: the beach, the beautiful people, and the parties... but exactly how long do you do this for?

We met at a beach party. We ended up dating for a few months afterwards.

Positives:
Tall, good-looking, cute personality, nice.

Negatives:
He tried to convince himself that he could deal with dating a "Mom"-- but he really couldn't.

What I learned:
Some men are still boys.

Frog #16

The "your mother would be so happy" frog

So, do you want to meet a nice Jewish Doctor?

We actually were introduced through my friend who dated him before I did, but it never worked out for them. I got over that and was willing to take her seconds if he was worth it! Hmm...I'm not sure is this working....is there something wrong with me?

Positives:
Good guy, smart, good looking, and who genuinely wanted a relationship with me. He really was a nice Jewish Doctor.

Negatives:
It just wasn't "there" for me.

What I learned:
You just can't explain chemistry (or lack thereof).

Frog #17

The "almost real deal" frog

Friends can turn into lovers.

This one previously dated one of my friends---you learn to get past that, (apparently New York City is not as big as you'd think).

What started out as a friendship turned into a serious 2-year relationship. We really enjoyed each other. It felt great to finally be part of a healthy couple. We had mutual respect, mutual attraction, and we loved each other. We even liked to do the same things... this was definitely "The One..."

Positives:

It was really nice having a boyfriend, and not having to date any more.

Negatives:

He, ultimately, was not ready to be a father to my son and couldn't make a commitment. This one threw me for a loop---I was really heart-broken and thought I'd never meet "The One."

What I learned:

I realized I didn't want to be with someone who was not ready to be an adult. I didn't mind it at the time but later on I realized how much I missed wearing high healed shoes.

Frog #18

The "good catch for someone else" frog

If at first you don't succeed, try, try again....

Since I was fortunate to have a lot of people who wanted to help me find someone, I often took advantage of it. So, when yet another friend asked if I wanted to meet someone, I said yes. This time I really liked the guy. He really seemed perfect at first. Good-looking, successful, smart, good personality...hmmm something must be wrong. Well, after a great start, it just fizzled out. Oh well, this just happens sometimes.

Positives:
I was so happy to have met a great guy after I had convinced myself that there were no great guys left.

Negatives:
He must not have felt the same way that I did.

What I learned:
It was good while it lasted. It helped me get over my last broken heart.

Side Note:
He ended up marrying a celebrity's daughter who shall also remain nameless (I sense a trend here).

Frog #19

The fun frog

Oh, come on we've all had at least one, right?

I hooked up with an old friend. We had a few fun nights together and some amusing phone calls.

Positives:
It was fun.

Negatives:
I knew he wasn't the "serious" type.

What I learned:
Never drink martinis on an empty stomach, an olive does not constitute dinner.

Frogs #20-?

You can actually go on too many dates.

I resisted, I refused, it was beneath me...eventually I gave in...and did it...the dreaded online dating.

Positives:

I met a lot of men…a few whom I was interested in. They say that "if you throw enough shit against the wall, something's bound to stick"… (my brother in law's expression) I think it's true.

Negatives:

People lie about their height, weight, age, income level and amount of hair they have. (Do they actually think you won't notice??)

What I learned:

You need a lot of time to devote to this to sort through all of the e-mails and decipher the good eggs from the bad. I felt like I needed a secretary to keep track of all the dates I was setting up. When it started feeling like a job, (one that I wasn't getting paid for or enjoying), I decided to take a break from it.

I'm So Over being green

Sometimes you just need a break from it all.

I stepped back and reevaluated myself, my life, and what I had to be proud of, and thankful for. I had my health, my great girl friends, my wonderful son, my career...maybe I didn't need a man after all.

I temporarily gave up searching for Mr. Right and bought a dog.

Positives:
I got unconditional love and affection.

Negatives:
He ruined the carpeting in my house and chewed a pair of my favorite boots. It's not fun walking a dog on a cold winter night.

What I learned:
Dogs really are the best companions. You can never be lonely when you have your dog with you.

In summation, after much Frog Handling

Sometimes I thought, was I too picky? No, no, no....I quickly came to my senses and remembered that we all deserve to be selective. Some people I know have spent more time picking out an outfit than they have in choosing a spouse. I look back on previous relationships and thank God that they didn't work out...I was so devastated when some of the men I dated didn't fall madly in love with me, or want to marry me, that I didn't stop to realize that they were not right for me in the first place, and that is exactly why it didn't work out.

Have I learned anything from all this dating? About myself? A great deal. About men? Well, let's just say I've learned what I like and what I don't like. But yes, men still sometimes confuse me.

Maybe we're not supposed to figure men out, but rather hope that we can find someone who will truly make us happy.

Maybe we can arrive at a place where we can overlook all that has bothered us about others, and instead, simply find someone who makes us laugh.

Maybe we stop looking, and trying so hard, and when we least expect it, the man who will fulfill all of our dreams will be right in front of us. It will be easy and natural. Because fate has a funny way of working things out. Hopefully, we will gain some wisdom along the way.

And, hopefully, with the help of my story, you'll enjoy kissing some of the frogs that hop into your life.

"When the right one comes along you will know it"

Is this the end of my stories from the lily pond?

The Prince.

No it is not. Actually, the final frog finally leapt into my world when I least expected it and changed my life.

Eight years after my divorce, (just as I became content and comfortable with being single), I met my soul mate and best friend. There was mutual attraction. There were no games. We made each other happy. It was honest and real from the very beginning. I guess that's how you know it is right. I was finally ready to share my life with someone special, (remember, timing is everything). Together, we have shared so much: good times and bad, challenges and achievements and laughter and tears.

In the end it was all worth it. I found myself, and then I found my prince, (warts and all!).

Top ten "must haves" for a single woman

1. A great little black dress (cliché but true)
2. Sexy shoes (same)
3. Comfortable shoes (you may be asked out on an outing)
4. A tool box with essential tools (everyone should know how to use a hammer and a screwdriver)
5. A gym membership (work out and be social at the same time)
6. A pet (so you will never feel lonely)
7. Wine (just keep in moderation)
8. Good books to read (nothing beats getting lost in a good book)
9. A comfortable home (so you are always happy there)
10. Good girl friends that make you laugh (priceless)

"If you surround yourself with things that make you happy, you will be happier"

Top ten "must dos" for a single woman

1. Join a club or take a class (having an interest makes you more interesting)
2. See lots of movies (it will always give you something to talk about on a date)
3. Don't feel sorry for yourself (it's unappealing)
4. Have friends over (it will make you feel appreciated)
5. Travel (if finances allow, you will grow from it)
6. Get manicures and pedicures (and other grooming essentials that will make you feel and look good)
7. Exercise (it will make you feel and look good)
8. Do a project in your home (you may really impress yourself)
9. Keep in touch with your friends and family (invaluable when you need a hand, an ear or a shoulder to cry on)
10. Volunteer for something (it will make you appreciate all the good things that you have in your life)

"If you are active,
you will be healthier"

Top ten "must learn" for a single woman

1. How to hang a picture (so you don't have to call an x-frog)
2. How to change a light bulb (it's too embarrassing if you really can't do it)
3. How to winterize the outside waterlines of your home or hire someone to do so (I learned my lesson when I had a flood in my house)
4. Where the circuit breakers are if you live in a house (so you don't have to call another x-frog)
5. How to cook dinner (it is true that a way to a man's heart is through his stomach)
6. To always have gas in your car and cash in your wallet (my father taught me that)
7. To keep an open mind
8. To take criticism
9. To not be so hard on yourself
10. To love yourself

"You must learn to love yourself
before someone else
can love you"

"You have to kiss
a lot of frogs..."

"Enjoy yourself while you explore the pond"

About The Author

Margo Fishler

Margo is happily living in Bucks County, Pennsylvania, a long way from the frog pond, with her husband, son, two stepdaughters, one stepson and her ever-faithful dog, Snowball. She loves being a wife, and is grateful to be a mother to all of her beautiful children. They give her inspiration each day, and continue to fill her life with joy. She keeps busy cultivating her career as a graphic designer, and working on several independent projects. This is Margo's first book.